An I Can Read Book®

The 18 PENNY GOOSE

story by Sally M. Walker

pictures by Ellen Beier

HarperTrophy®
A Division of HarperCollins*Publishers*

The 18 Penny Goose

Library of Congress Cataloging-in-Publication Data
Walker, Sally M.
The 18 penny goose / story by Sally M. Walker ; pictures by Ellen Beier Curtis.
p. cm. — (An I can read book)
Summary: Eight-year-old Letty attempts to save her pet goose from marauding British soldiers in New Jersey during the Revolutionary War.
ISBN 0-06-027556-1. — ISBN 0-06-027557-X (lib. bdg.)
ISBN 0-06-444250-0 (pbk.)
1. New Jersey—History—Revolution, 1775–1783—Juvenile fiction. [1.New Jersey—History—Revolution, 1775–1783—Fiction. 2. United States—History—Revolution, 1775–1783—Fiction. 3. Geese—Fiction.] I. Beier, Ellen, ill. II. Title. III. Series.
PZ7.W153845Aah 1998 96-46229
[E]—dc21 CIP
AC

First Harper Trophy edition, 1999

Visit us on the World Wide Web!
http://www.harperchildrens.com

For Undough, Nell, and Thayo.
Stories hide in the history of every town.
They wait for us to find them.
—S.M.W.

To Rosella, with thanks
—E.B.

Contents

Chapter One · Run and Hide

It was the spring of 1778.

Letty Wright ran across the barnyard.

British soldiers

were only a mile or two away.

They were marching

toward Letty's house.

Letty's family had to leave quickly
and go over the mountain,
where they would be safe.
But first,
Letty had to warn
her flock of geese.

"Shoo, Solomon. You foolish goose!
Take your wives and hide!"
Letty waved her arms
at the gander.
"Hurry, Letty!" called Ma.

Ma was ready to go.

She handed baby Sarah up to Pa.

Letty's brother, John, peeked

over the side of the wagon.

He was sucking his thumb.

He did that only when he was afraid.

Letty's legs shook.

Her stomach felt sick.

She could hear rifles shooting.

The British were getting closer.

"Please, Solomon," Letty said,
"you must hide
while the soldiers are here.
Hide in the woods
where they won't see you!
It will only be for a few days.
Our soldiers will come
and chase the British away.
Then you can come home."

Solomon honked at Letty.
He flapped his wings
and ran across the yard.
But he did not hide.
"Letty, get in the wagon.
We must go now.
Solomon must take care of himself,"
said Ma.
"Wait, please!" Letty begged.
Letty knew soldiers stole things
and took farm animals for food.
She had to save
Solomon and the other geese.

Dear Soldiers
Please do not
my geese

Letty ran into the house.

She grabbed a sheet of paper

and a quill pen and wrote:

Dear Soldiers,

Please do not harm my geese.

Solomon, the gander, is my friend.

I raised him from a baby.

He knows you are coming,

but he will not run away and hide.

Thank you,

Letty Wright, age 8.

Letty put the letter

on the mantel.

Maybe the soldiers

would read her note.

Maybe, just maybe,

they would not hurt her geese.

Letty ran outside.

Pa pulled her up into the wagon.

At the bend in the road,
Letty looked back.
She was afraid
she would never see her home
or Solomon again.

Chapter Two · Over the Mountain

"Where will we sleep?"

asked Letty.

"We will stay with Pa's friends,"

said Ma.

"They have a big barn.

We will be safe there."

The two cows were tied
behind the wagon.
They mooed and mooed.

“The dust hurts their eyes,”

said John.

“My eyes hurt too,” said Letty.

She blinked away tears

and looked at Pa.

"Will the soldiers burn our house?"

asked Letty.

"Will they take Solomon

and his wives?"

"I hope not," said Pa.

His face was grim.

"I wrote a letter to the soldiers.

I asked them not to hurt my geese,"

said Letty.

Pa shook his head.

"I will not lie to you, Letty.

If the soldiers are hungry,

they will take your geese,"

said Pa.

Letty closed her eyes tightly
and said nothing.
Ma held Letty's hand.

The Wrights' wagon rolled past
the Chapmans' house.
The Chapmans' horses were gone.
Letty's friend Jemima
and her family had already left.

Letty was glad the British soldiers
would not get the Chapmans' horses.
She was glad Pa had tied their cows
to the wagon.
She wished there had been time
to catch Solomon and his wives.

When they got to the top
of the mountain,
Letty looked down.
She could hear guns.
She could see smoke.
She could not see her house.
She could not see Solomon.

Chapter Three · Waiting

Letty and her family
stayed with Pa's friends
for three days.
Jemima's family was there too.

During the day,
Letty milked her family's cows.
She fed the chickens
that lived on the farm,
but they were not as friendly
as Solomon and his wives.

At night,

everyone slept in the barn.

Each evening,

Letty wished on the first star.

She wished her home would be safe.

She wished Solomon would be safe.

Everyone kept talking
about the British soldiers.

Jemima said,
"My pa said that British soldiers
knew Mistress Crane was sick.
They stole her feather bed anyway,
because they wanted
a soft place to sleep!"
Thinking about feather beds
made Letty sad.
Hearing about mean soldiers
made her feel even worse.
The soldiers would laugh
at her letter
and eat Solomon for dinner.

On the third day,
an American soldier
rode up to the house.

“Our soldiers have chased
the British away.
They will not come back.
You may go home,” he said.

Pa got the wagon ready.

Jemima hugged Letty.

“I hope Solomon is all right,”

said Jemima.

“Come and visit me

as soon as you can,” said Letty.

Pa helped Letty into the wagon.

Letty and her family headed home.

Chapter Four · Home Again

The Wrights' wagon
passed the Chapmans' house.
"The soldiers did not burn
Jemima's house," said Letty.
"The Chapmans were lucky," said Pa.

He clucked to the horse.

The wagon wheels turned faster.

“I hope we are lucky,” said Ma.

Letty crossed her fingers.

Soon they reached

the bend in the road.

"Thank goodness," said Ma.

The house was not burned.

But the fences were broken,

and Ma's garden was trampled.

Worst of all, the geese were gone!

"Solomon . . ." Letty started to cry.

The Wrights went into the house.

Ma cried when she stepped inside.

Her spinning wheel was broken.

Smashed dishes were on the floor.

The soldiers had hammered

metal spikes into the mantel

and roasted food on them.

"Look," Pa said.

He took something from the mantel.

"A letter for you, Letty.

It is from the British soldiers."

Letty read the letter:

Dear Mistress Wright,

We must bid you good-night,

it is time for us to wander.

We have paid for your geese,

a penny a piece,

and left the change

with the gander."

Letty dropped the letter
and ran outside.
"Solomon . . . Solomon,
where are you?"
called Letty.

“Honk, honk!”

Solomon waddled out of the barn.

A leather sack

was tied around his neck.

“Oh, Solomon,” cried Letty.

“You are safe.”

Letty hugged him.

She opened the sack.
Eighteen English pennies
spilled into her hand.
Letty looked at the pennies.
She looked at Solomon.
"I am sorry about your wives,"
said Letty.
"We will help him find new ones,"
said Ma and Pa.
"Even if this is British money,
these are lucky pennies,"
said Letty.

"Our house was not burned,"
Letty said.
"Solomon is safe,
and the soldiers are gone."
Letty walked back to the house
with her family.
There was a lot of work to be done.
And Letty was glad to do it.

Author's Note

THE 18 PENNY GOOSE is based on a true story. The Wright family lived in New Jersey, in the area now known as East Orange. British soldiers on foraging raids rode across the countryside surrounding the Wrights' farm several times during 1778. They raided homesteads, destroyed property, and stole cattle, horses, hay, and food.

When the Wright family returned from their flight, they did indeed find the British soldiers' note that was included in the story. The tobacco sack tied around the gander's neck contained eighteen English pennies, with the words *Georgius Rex*, which means King George, stamped on them. Descendants of the Wright family still had eleven of the coins in their possession more than 150 years later.

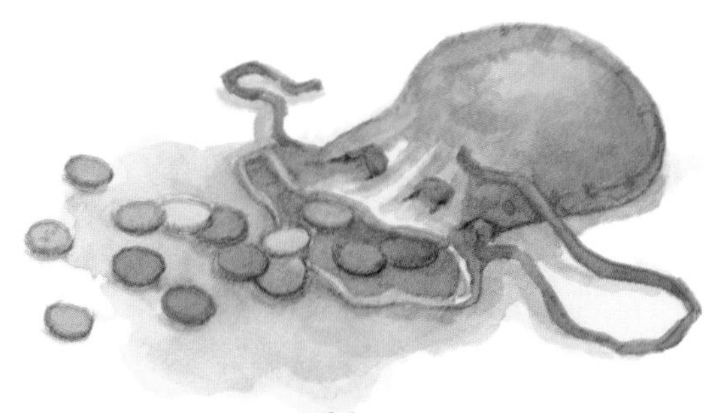

Sally M. Walker first discovered Letty Wright's story as an elementary school student researching local history. Since then, she has written many science books for children, including RHINOS and EARTHQUAKES, a CBC/NSTA Outstanding Science Trade Book of 1997. Ms. Walker is a children's literature consultant and lives in DeKalb, Illinois.

Ellen Beier's illustrations appear in a number of children's books, most recently THE BLUE HILL MEADOWS by Cynthia Rylant. Having lived in Europe for several years, Ms. Beier and her family now live in Red Wing, Minnesota.